LITTI
and tl

Constance Boyle

Woodbury, New York · London · Toronto · Sydney

First U.S. edition published in 1985 by
Barron's Educational Series, Inc.
© Constance Boyle 1985

This book has been designed and produced by
Aurum Press Ltd., 33 Museum Street,
London WC1A 1LD, England

All inquiries should be addressed to:
Barron's Educational Series, Inc.
113 Crossways Park Drive
Woodbury, New York 11797

International Standard Book No. 0-8120-5639-6
Library of Congress Catalog Card No.

PRINTED IN BELGIUM
5 6 7 8   9 8 7 6 5 4 3 2 1

When Little Owl was small, he often helped in the garden.

Little Owl's brother Olly liked to help, too.

Daddy let Little Owl try most things in
the garden. He wouldn't let him help
with the seedlings, though. "They're
too delicate," he said.

But he was always glad of Little Owl's help with the digging.

They both had boots for this sort of work.

They had to be very careful about
mud . . .

. . . and, to help, they had a great big doormat outside on the step.

One day, in the early spring, Little Owl
noticed a bit of green in the corner of
the doormat, by the wall.

It was a tiny
seedling,
growing all
by itself!

Little Owl was very excited. He
fetched his mother to look.

"We can't have weeds growing in the
doormat!" she cried. "Whatever would
Daddy say?" But she didn't pull it up.

"Dad says you can keep your weed," announced Olly next day. "It can't last long, anyway, on a dry mat."

Little Owl was a bit upset. He went off and got his watering can and a bag of plant food out of the shed.

The doormat was **VERY** wet when he had finished.

"This weed of Little Owl's is growing very fast," remarked Daddy, a week or two later.

"He keeps watering it," said Mommy.

Olly noticed, too.
He thought the
weed was a real
joke, and started
jumping over it.

As the weed grew
bigger, life in the
kitchen . . .

. . . got quite exciting!

One day, when the sun was warmer,
Little Owl took his teddy and his own
garden chair and sat by his weed on the
back step.

There wasn't much room on the top
step, and the chair slipped over the
edge.

Little Owl landed
on his head, at the
bottom of the
steps.

"This is really silly!" said his mother.
"You mustn't sit in such a dangerous
place again."

"Hello, what's happened?" asked Daddy, coming in.

"He fell down the steps," answered Mommy.

But nothing could
stop . . .

Little
Owl . . .

from taking care
of his weed.

"I can hardly get in the door!" said
Daddy. "We'll HAVE to get rid of it!"
"But you promised Little Owl," said
Mommy.

But, at last . . .

"This is IMPOSSIBLE!" exclaimed
Daddy, struggling with the weed.
"Yes, I know," said Mommy.

Next morning,
Little Owl went
off to spend the
whole day with his
cousin, Henrietta.

He told her
all about his
weed, and she
promised to
come and
see it.

The following day, when Little Owl opened the door to go out into the garden, there was a new doormat on the step. The weed had gone.

He was terribly upset.

"It's all right, Chick," said his mother.
"Go and find Daddy. He's in the
garden."

Little Owl went sadly through the garden, and there at the end was the weed!

It was still growing in its doormat, and looked very much alive.

Little Owl could hardly believe it!

"It would soon have died on the step,"
said Daddy. "There's plenty of earth
for it here."

So Little Owl stopped giving it plant food, and it stopped getting bigger.

"What a relief! I really thought it was going to take over!" said Daddy.

This is what he had imagined.

Everyone started to like the weed
when it was away from the house.

Daddy trimmed it a bit, and
on Mommy's birthday
Henrietta came to supper,
and they had a picnic
in the garden.

"How lovely! A birthday party under a tree!" said Mommy.
"A real tree!" thought Little Owl, happily.